for the Book with
my dad. It's a winner.

C c

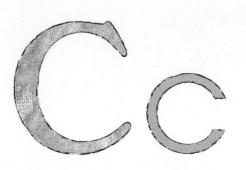

for the Clock that
tick-tocks on the wall.

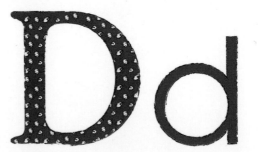

D d

is my Dog, who's
not sleepy at all.

 Ee

is for Ears, tucked
warm out of sight,

  Ff

for my Fingers,
holding on tight.

Gg

is for Gran,

with an

Hh

for her Hug.

She tucks me in tight like a bug in a rug.

I i

is for Insect
asleep in its nook.

J j

for my Jacket and
Jeans on their hook.

K k

is a Kiss on the
cheek from my mom.

L l

is for Lullaby ...
dom di-di dom.

Mm

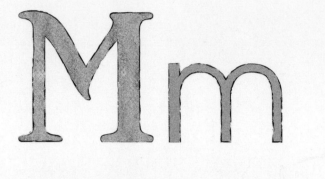

is for Moon shining
bright through the lace.

Nn

for my Nose on the
front of my face.

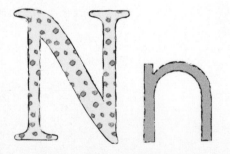

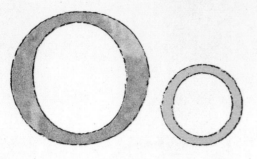

for the Owl
outside in the tree.

for Pajamas.
Now shake my foot free.

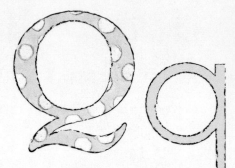 

is for Quiet,

and

for my Room.

Lit by my night-light that glows in the gloom.

S s

is for Sandman and
Sleep in my eyes.

T t

for my Teddy, who's
here till sunrise.

Uu

is for Under
the covers I creep.

Vv

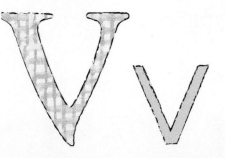

is for Vanishing ...
almost asleep.

W w

Whispering
prayers for us all.

X x

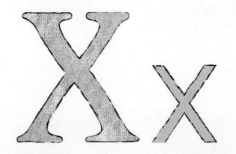

for relaX, now I'm
facing the wall.

Yy is for Yawn, and
I'm ready for sleep.

All hushed until morning.
You won't hear a peep.

Zz

Z ... Z ... Z ... Z ...

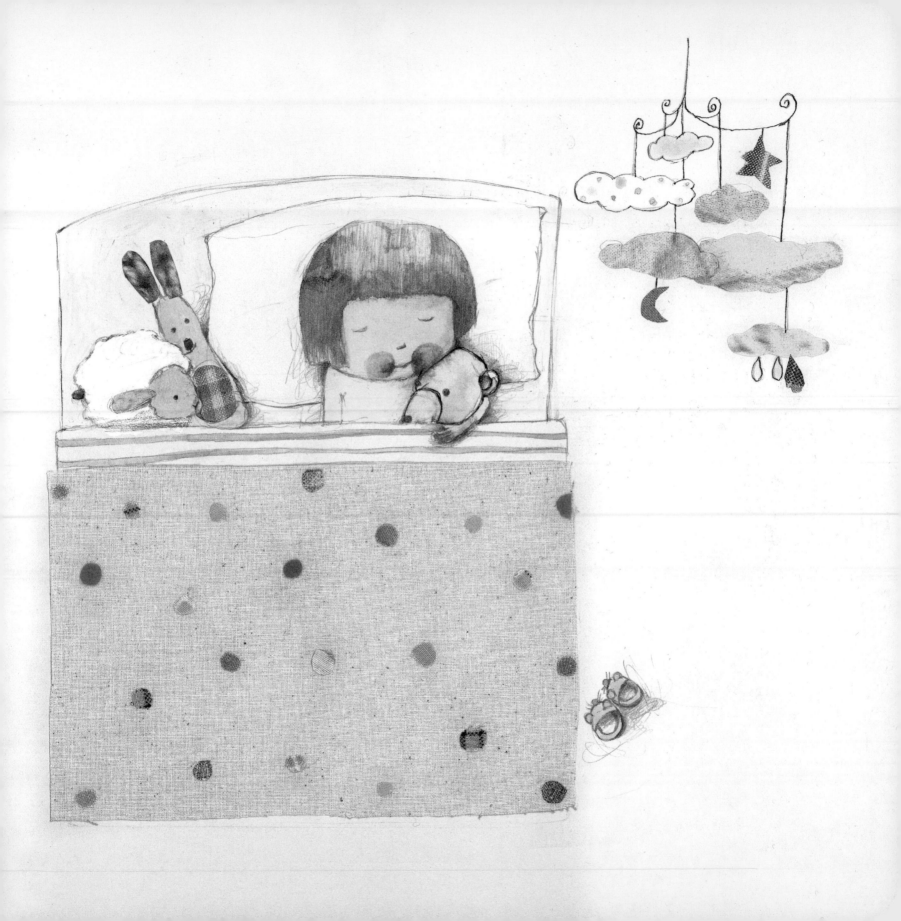

Good night!